To

- -

From

- -

With thanks to Jane Horne.

Copyright © 2008

make believe ideas

27 Castle Street, Berkhamsted,
Hertfordshire, HP4 2DW.

Manufactured in China

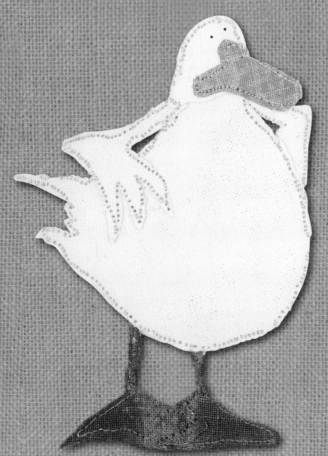

DUCKIE DUCK

KATE TOMS

make
believe
ideas

Quack Quack Quack

Most ducks quack

as they waddle along

The other little ducks
all love to swim

but not Duckie—
a boat is best
for him!

Ducks all waddle
when they go
to the shop.

Not Duckie of course: he likes to hop.

The ducks
eat grass
at dinnertime.

In a frenzy of flapping,
ducks take to the sky,

while **Duckie's balloon** floats quietly by.

Feathers fly when the ducks spy a fox...

but Duckie stands firm, as strong as an ox!

The ducks hurry home when day turns to night . . .

but
Duckie goes out
with a bright
flashlight!

At night,
the ducks gather
in the warmth of
their shed,

while the branch of a tree is Duckie's bed!

while Duckie goes
exploring in his sporty
little car.

Heads in the water,

1, 2, 3!

Quack

Quack Quack

Duckie says,
"NO! That's not for me!"

but for Duckie, being different is what he likes best!

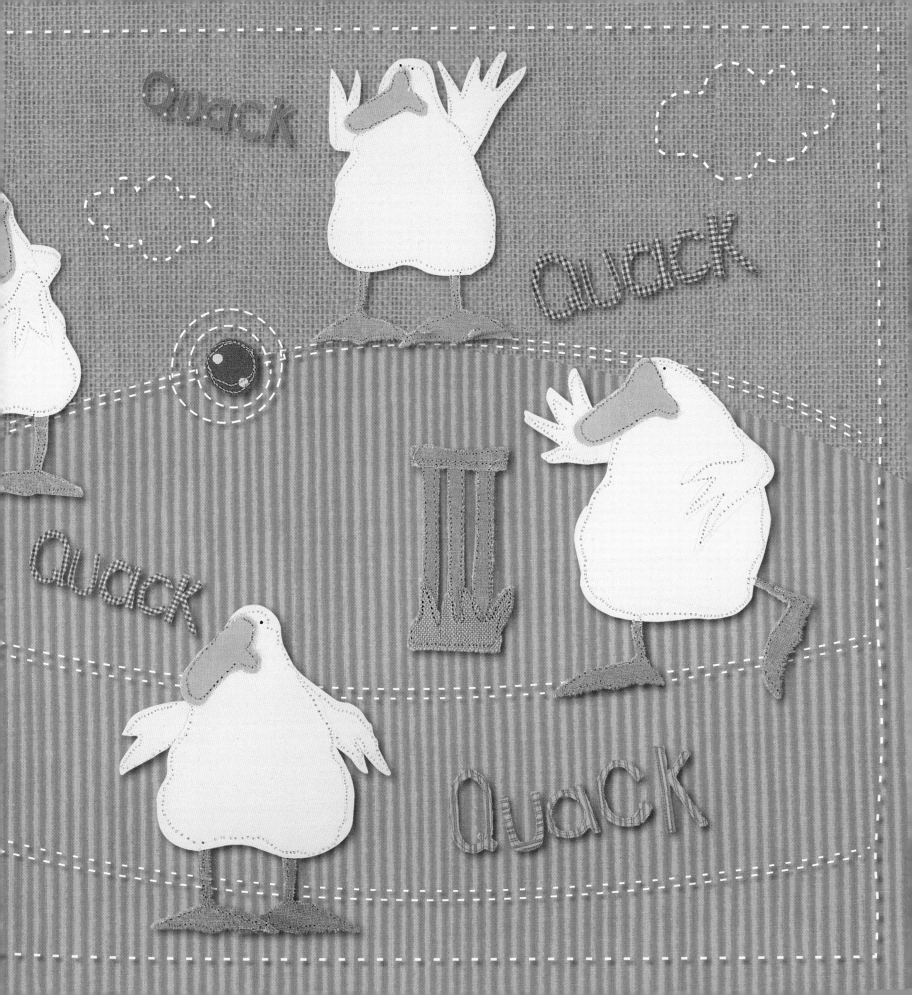